For Real, I PARADED IN MY UNDERPANTS!

The Story of

EMP...
NEW...

AS TO...
EMI...

by **Nancy Loewen**

illustrated by **Russ Cox**

Raintree is an imprint of Capstone Global Library Limited, a company incorporated in England and Wales having its registered office at 264 Banbury Road, Oxford, OX2 7DY – Registered company number: 6695582

www.raintree.co.uk
myorders@raintree.co.uk

Editor: Jill Kalz
Designer: Lori Bye
Premedia Specialist: Tori Abraham

The illustrations in this book were created digitally.
Original illustrations © Capstone Global Library Limited 2018
Originated by Capstone Global Library Limited

ISBN 978 1 4747 5342 5
22 21 20 19 18
10 9 8 7 6 5 4 3 2 1

British Library Cataloguing in Publication Data
A full catalogue record for this book is available from the British Library.

Printed and bound in India.

My name is Emperor Twill, ruler of the kingdom Pardonia.

Did you just giggle? Did I hear a snort? Well, I should be used to it. After all, I'm the fool who marched down the streets of his city wearing nothing but his underpants.

But I have to say, that totally embarrassing parade helped me save my kingdom. So please, stop your sniggering and let me tell you *my* side of the story!

A while back, the Kingdom of Pardonia had a real problem. People were **TOO NICE**.

We had traffic jams every single day. Everyone wanted to let the *other* driver go first.

Losing teams would always get "one more chance". Ball games went on and on, until the players fell asleep.

People didn't want to hurt anyone's feelings, so they didn't say what they really thought. That led to some very bad ideas.

A water park for cats? Bad idea.

Tarantula Day? Bad idea.

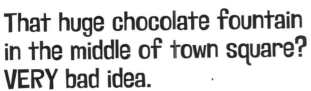

That huge chocolate fountain in the middle of town square? VERY bad idea.

Yes, I could have stepped in. But when everyone else is always smiling and agreeing, it can be hard to speak up. Even for an emperor.

7

The day the town square closed because of all the flies, I knew it was time to make some changes.

I couldn't do it all by myself. So I set about finding someone who could help me turn my kingdom into a nice but **REASONABLE** place.

8

One day two tailors appeared at my palace. They offered to make me the finest outfit one could ever hope to see.

They weren't really tailors, though. They were actors! Their names were Walton and Skeet – and I'd hired them myself. It was a test, you see. I asked the actors to pretend to make me invisible clothes. I wanted to see if any of my advisors would be bold enough to say something.

Walton and Skeet "worked" day and night.

I checked in on them every so often and loudly praised their work. "So many colours!" I would say. "And the pattern – so enchanting!"

My advisors squinted and scratched their heads.

"What do you think?" I asked my first advisor.

Little beads of sweat popped up on his brow. "Um . . . ah . . . er . . . it's very fine work indeed!" he said.

"And you?" I asked my second advisor.

He bit his lip nervously. "Words can't describe it!" he replied.

One by one I asked all of my advisors to tell me what they thought of the amazing cloth. Not one of them told me the truth. They were too afraid of hurting my feelings!

Soon Walton and Skeet started "sewing" the clothes. During a fitting, they pretended to fuss with a jacket, robe and trousers that weren't there. And no one said a thing except "ooohhh" and "aaahhh".

Surely **SOMEONE** in the kingdom knew how to speak up.

I had to find that person. And I knew what had to be done.

14

I made plans for a grand parade. We had musicians, horses, jugglers, acrobats . . . and finally there was me. Me, Emperor Twill of Pardonia, marching down the street in my underpants.

As I went by, people stared. But they clapped and bowed, just like always.

Would **NO ONE** speak up? Was I embarrassing myself for no reason?

Suddenly a child's voice rose from the crowd.

"But he hasn't got anything on!" it said.

I stopped in my tracks.

"Who said that?" I shouted.

"Me, I did! It was me!" came the voice again.

I made my way through the crowd, so eager to meet this brave child that I somehow forgot all about my clothes-less condition. Walton threw me a robe. A **REAL** robe.

My outspoken hero was a young girl. Grown-ups bobbed around her with whispers of "shhh!" and "say you're sorry!" I waved them away.

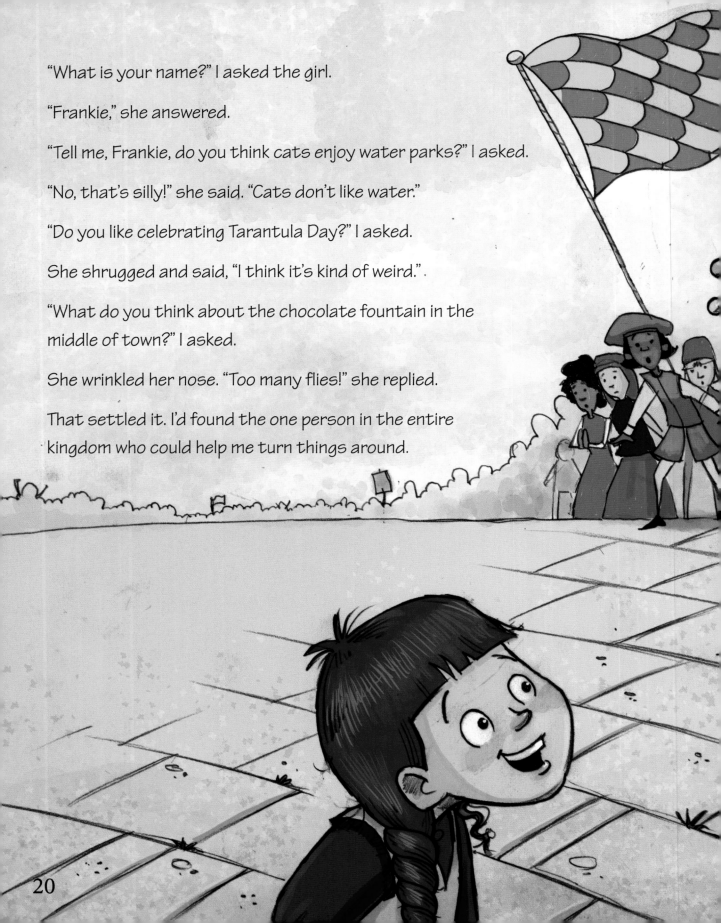

"What is your name?" I asked the girl.

"Frankie," she answered.

"Tell me, Frankie, do you think cats enjoy water parks?" I asked.

"No, that's silly!" she said. "Cats don't like water."

"Do you like celebrating Tarantula Day?" I asked.

She shrugged and said, "I think it's kind of weird."

"What do you think about the chocolate fountain in the middle of town?" I asked.

She wrinkled her nose. "Too many flies!" she replied.

That settled it. I'd found the one person in the entire kingdom who could help me turn things around.

Thanks to Frankie, Pardonia is starting to make a lot more sense.

Ball games end when they're supposed to. Traffic flows freely. Tarantula Day has been replaced with Doughnut Day.

And now that the chocolate fountain is gone, we have just a normal amount of flies.

So you see, I'm not a fool. I was *brave* to do what I did.

And now everyone in Pardonia can be a little braver too.

Think about it

What problems did the kingdom of Pardonia face because its people were "too nice"?

Why did Emperor Twill hire actors and pretend to see clothes that weren't there? What was his goal?

On page 12, when the advisor says, "Um . . . ah . . . er . . .", what does that tell us about how he was feeling?

Look online to find the original "The Emperor's New Clothes" story. How is the character of Emperor Twill in this version different from the emperor in the original story? Describe how the plots are alike and how they are different.

This story is told from the emperor's point of view. If Frankie were telling this story, what details would be different? How about if Walton and Skeet told the story? Or one of the emperor's advisors?

Glossary

character person, animal or creature in a story
plot what happens in a story
point of view way of looking at something
version account of something from a certain point of view

Find out more

Books

An Illustrated Treasury of Hans Christian Andersen's Fairy Tales
(Floris Books, 2014)

The Emperor's New Clothes, Susie Day (Collins, 2017)

Website

**www.bbc.co.uk/learning/schoolradio/subjects/
english/hans_christian_andersen/tales**
Visit this website to listen to some of the fairy tales
written by Hans Christian Andersen.

Look for all the books in the series:

Believe Me, Goldilocks Rocks!

Believe Me, I Never Felt a Pea!

For Real, I Paraded in My Underpants!

Frankly, I'd Rather Spin Myself a New Name!

Frankly, I Never Wanted to Kiss Anybody!

Honestly, Our Music Stole the Show!

Honestly, Red Riding Hood Was Rotten!

Listen, My Bridge Is SO Cool!

No Kidding, Mermaids Are a Joke!

No Lie, I Acted Like a Beast!

No Lie, Pigs (and Their Houses) CAN Fly!

Really, Rapunzel Needed a Haircut!

Seriously, Cinderella Is SO Annoying!

Seriously, Snow White Was SO Forgetful!

Truly, We Both Loved Beauty Dearly!

Trust Me, Hansel and Gretel Are SWEET!

Trust Me, Jack's Beanstalk Stinks!

Truthfully, Something Smelled Fishy!